Overruled

George Bernard Shaw

Contents

OVERRULED

BY

George Bernard Shaw

PREFACE TO OVERRULED.

THE ALLEVIATIONS OF MONOGAMY.

This piece is not an argument for or against polygamy. It is a clinical study of how the thing actually occurs among quite ordinary people, innocent of all unconventional views concerning it. The enormous majority of cases in real life are those of people in that position. Those who deliberately and conscientiously profess what are oddly called advanced views by those others who believe them to be retrograde, are often, and indeed mostly, the last people in the world to engage in unconventional adventures of any kind, not only because they have neither time nor disposition for them, but because the friction set up between the individual and the community by the expression of unusual views of any sort is quite enough hindrance to the heretic without being complicated by personal scandals. Thus the theoretic libertine is usually a person of blameless family life, whilst the practical libertine is mercilessly severe on all other libertines, and excessively conventional in professions of social principle.

What is more, these professions are not hypocritical: they are for the most part quite sincere. The common libertine, like the drunkard, succumbs to a temptation which he does not defend, and against which he warns others with an earnestness proportionate to the intensity of his own remorse. He (or she) may be a liar and a humbug, pretending to be better than the detected libertines, and clamoring for their condign punishment; but this is mere self-defence. No reasonable person expects the burglar to confess his pursuits, or to refrain from joining in the cry of Stop Thief when the police get on the track of another burglar. If society chooses to penalize candor, it has itself to thank if its attack is countered by falsehood. The clamorous virtue of the libertine is therefore no more hypocritical than the plea of Not Guilty which is allowed to every criminal. But one result is that the theorists who write most sincerely and favorably about polygamy know least about it; and the practitioners who know most about it keep their knowledge very jealously to themselves. Which is hardly fair to the practice.

INACCESSIBILITY OF THE FACTS.

Also it is impossible to estimate its prevalence. A practice to which nobody confesses may be both universal and unsuspected, just as a virtue which everybody is expected, under heavy penalties, to claim, may have no existence. It is often assumed--indeed it is the official assumption of the Churches and the divorce courts that a gentleman and a lady cannot be alone together innocently. And that is manifest blazing nonsense, though many women have been stoned to death in the east, and divorced in the west, on the strength of it. On the other hand, the innocent and conventional people who regard the gallant adventures as crimes of so horrible a nature that only the most depraved and desperate characters engage in them or would listen to advances in that direction without raising an alarm with the noisiest indignation, are clearly examples of the fact that most sections of society do not know how the other sections live. Industry is the most effective check on gallantry. Women may, as Napoleon said, be the occupation of the idle man just as men are the preoccupation of the idle woman; but the mass of mankind is too busy and too poor for the long and expensive sieges which the professed libertine lays to virtue. Still, wherever there is idleness or even a reasonable supply of elegant leisure there is a good deal of coquetry and philandering. It is so much pleasanter to dance on the edge of a precipice than to go over it that leisured society is full of people who spend a great part of their lives in flirtation, and conceal nothing but the humiliating secret that they have never gone any further. For there is no pleasing people in the matter of reputation in this department: every insult is a flattery; every testimonial is a disparagement: Joseph is despised and promoted, Potiphar's wife admired and condemned: in short, you are never on solid ground until you get away from the subject altogether. There is a continual and irreconcilable conflict between the natural and conventional sides of the case, between spontaneous human relations between independent men and women on the one hand and the property relation between husband and wife on the other, not to mention the confusion under the common name of love of a generous natural attraction and interest with the murderous jealousy that fastens on and clings to its mate (especially a hated mate) as a tiger fastens on a carcase. And the confusion is natural; for these extremes are extremes of the same passion; and most cases lie somewhere on the scale between them, and are so complicated by ordinary likes and dislikes, by incidental wounds to vanity or gratifications of it, and by class feeling, that A will be jealous of B and not of C, and will tolerate infidelities on the part of D whilst being furiously angry when they are committed by E.

THE CONVENTION OF JEALOUSY

That jealousy is independent of sex is shown by its intensity in children, and by the fact that very jealous people are jealous of everybody without regard to relationship or sex, and cannot bear to hear the person they "love" speak favorably of anyone under any circumstances (many women, for instance, are much more jealous of their husbands' mothers and sisters than of unrelated women whom they suspect

him of fancying); but it is seldom possible to disentangle the two
passions in practice. Besides, jealousy is an inculcated passion,
forced by society on people in whom it would not occur spontaneously.
In Brieux's Bourgeois aux Champs, the benevolent hero finds himself
detested by the neighboring peasants and farmers, not because he
preserves game, and sets mantraps for poachers, and defends his legal
rights over his land to the extremest point of unsocial savagery, but
because, being an amiable and public-spirited person, he refuses to do
all this, and thereby offends and disparages the sense of property in
his neighbors. The same thing is true of matrimonial jealousy; the man
who does not at least pretend to feel it and behave as badly as if he
really felt it is despised and insulted; and many a man has shot or
stabbed a friend or been shot or stabbed by him in a duel, or disgraced
himself and ruined his own wife in a divorce scandal, against his
conscience, against his instinct, and to the destruction of his home,
solely because Society conspired to drive him to keep its own lower
morality in countenance in this miserable and undignified manner.

Morality is confused in such matters. In an elegant plutocracy, a
jealous husband is regarded as a boor. Among the tradesmen who supply
that plutocracy with its meals, a husband who is not jealous, and
refrains from assailing his rival with his fists, is regarded as a
ridiculous, contemptible and cowardly cuckold. And the laboring class
is divided into the respectable section which takes the tradesman's
view, and the disreputable section which enjoys the license of the
plutocracy without its money: creeping below the law as its exemplars
prance above it; cutting down all expenses of respectability and even
decency; and frankly accepting squalor and disrepute as the price of
anarchic self-indulgence. The conflict between Malvolio and Sir Toby,
between the marquis and the bourgeois, the cavalier and the puritan,
the ascetic and the voluptuary, goes on continually, and goes on not
only between class and class and individual and individual, but in the
selfsame breast in a series of reactions and revulsions in which the

irresistible becomes the unbearable, and the unbearable the
irresistible, until none of us can say what our characters really are
in this respect.

THE MISSING DATA OF A SCIENTIFIC NATURAL HISTORY OF MARRIAGE.

Of one thing I am persuaded: we shall never attain to a reasonable
healthy public opinion on sex questions until we offer, as the data for
that opinion, our actual conduct and our real thoughts instead of a
moral fiction which we agree to call virtuous conduct, and which we
then--and here comes in the mischief--pretend is our conduct and our
thoughts. If the result were that we all believed one another to be
better than we really are, there would be something to be said for it;
but the actual result appears to be a monstrous exaggeration of the
power and continuity of sexual passion. The whole world shares the fate
of Lucrezia Borgia, who, though she seems on investigation to have been
quite a suitable wife for a modern British Bishop, has been invested by
the popular historical imagination with all the extravagances of a
Messalina or a Cenci. Writers of belles lettres who are rash enough to
admit that their whole life is not one constant preoccupation with
adored members of the opposite sex, and who even countenance La
Rochefoucauld's remark that very few people would ever imagine
themselves in love if they had never read anything about it, are
gravely declared to be abnormal or physically defective by critics of
crushing unadventurousness and domestication. French authors of saintly
temperament are forced to include in their retinue countesses of ardent
complexion with whom they are supposed to live in sin. Sentimental
controversies on the subject are endless; but they are useless, because
nobody tells the truth. Rousseau did it by an extraordinary effort,
aided by a superhuman faculty for human natural history, but the result

was curiously disconcerting because, though the facts were so conventionally shocking that people felt that they ought to matter a great deal, they actually mattered very little. And even at that everybody pretends not to believe him.

ARTIFICIAL RETRIBUTION.

The worst of that is that busybodies with perhaps rather more than a normal taste for mischief are continually trying to make negligible things matter as much in fact as they do in convention by deliberately inflicting injuries--sometimes atrocious injuries--on the parties concerned. Few people have any knowledge of the savage punishments that are legally inflicted for aberrations and absurdities to which no sanely instructed community would call any attention. We create an artificial morality, and consequently an artificial conscience, by manufacturing disastrous consequences for events which, left to themselves, would do very little harm (sometimes not any) and be forgotten in a few days.

But the artificial morality is not therefore to be condemned offhand. In many cases it may save mischief instead of making it: for example, though the hanging of a murderer is the duplication of a murder, yet it may be less murderous than leaving the matter to be settled by blood feud or vendetta. As long as human nature insists on revenge, the official organization and satisfaction of revenge by the State may be also its minimization. The mischief begins when the official revenge persists after the passion it satisfies has died out of the race. Stoning a woman to death in the east because she has ventured to marry again after being deserted by her husband may be more merciful than allowing her to be mobbed to death; but the official stoning or burning of an adulteress in the west would be an atrocity because few of us hate an adulteress to the extent of desiring such a penalty, or of being prepared to take the law into our own hands if it were withheld. Now what applies to this extreme case applies also in due degree to the other cases. Offences in which sex is concerned are often needlessly magnified by penalties, ranging from various forms of social ostracism to long sentences of penal servitude, which would be seen to be monstrously disproportionate to the real feeling against them if the removal of both the penalties and the taboo on their discussion made it possible for us to ascertain their real prevalence and estimation. Fortunately there is one outlet for the truth. We are permitted to discuss in jest what we may not discuss in earnest. A serious comedy about sex is taboo: a farcical comedy is privileged.

THE FAVORITE SUBJECT OF FARCICAL COMEDY.

The little piece which follows this preface accordingly takes the form of a farcical comedy, because it is a contribution to the very extensive dramatic literature which takes as its special department the gallantries of married people. The stage has been preoccupied by such affairs for centuries, not only in the jesting vein of Restoration Comedy and Palais Royal farce, but in the more tragically turned adulteries of the Parisian school which dominated the stage until Ibsen put them out of countenance and relegated them to their proper place as articles of commerce. Their continued vogue in that department maintains the tradition that adultery is the dramatic subject par excellence, and indeed that a play that is not about adultery is not a play at all. I was considered a heresiarch of the most extravagant kind when I expressed my opinion at the outset of my career as a playwright, that adultery is the dullest of themes on the stage, and that from Francesca and Paolo down to the latest guilty couple of the school of Dumas fils, the romantic adulterers have all been intolerable bores.

THE PSEUDO SEX PLAY.

Later on, I had occasion to point out to the defenders of sex as the proper theme of drama, that though they were right in ranking sex as an intensely interesting subject, they were wrong in assuming that sex is an indispensable motive in popular plays. The plays of Moliere are, like the novels of the Victorian epoch or Don Quixote, as nearly sexless as anything not absolutely inhuman can be; and some of Shakespear's plays are sexually on a par with the census: they contain women as well as men, and that is all. This had to be admitted; but it was still assumed that the plays of the XIX century Parisian school are, in contrast with the sexless masterpieces, saturated with sex; and this I strenuously denied. A play about the convention that a man should fight a duel or come to fisticuffs with his wife's lover if she has one, or the convention that he should strangle her like Othello, or turn her out of the house and never see her or allow her to see her children again, or the convention that she should never be spoken to again by any decent person and should finally drown herself, or the convention that persons involved in scenes of recrimination or confession by these conventions should call each other certain abusive names and describe their conduct as guilty and frail and so on: all these may provide material for very effective plays; but such plays are not dramatic studies of sex: one might as well say that Romeo and Juliet is a dramatic study of pharmacy because the catastrophe is brought about through an apothecary. Duels are not sex; divorce cases are not sex; the Trade Unionism of married women is not sex. Only the most insignificant fraction of the gallantries of married people produce any of the conventional results; and plays occupied wholly with the conventional results are therefore utterly unsatisfying as sex plays, however interesting they may be as plays of intrigue and plot puzzles.

The world is finding this out rapidly. The Sunday papers, which in the days when they appealed almost exclusively to the lower middle class were crammed with police intelligence, and more especially with divorce and murder cases, now lay no stress on them; and police papers which confined themselves entirely to such matters, and were once eagerly read, have perished through the essential dulness of their topics. And yet the interest in sex is stronger than ever: in fact, the literature that has driven out the journalism of the divorce courts is a literature occupied with sex to an extent and with an intimacy and frankness that would have seemed utterly impossible to Thackeray or Dickens if they had been told that the change would complete itself within fifty years of their own time.

ART AND MORALITY.

It is ridiculous to say, as inconsiderate amateurs of the arts do, that art has nothing to do with morality. What is true is that the artist's business is not that of the policeman; and that such factitious consequences and put-up jobs as divorces and executions and the detective operations that lead up to them are no essential part of life, though, like poisons and buttered slides and red-hot pokers, they provide material for plenty of thrilling or amusing stories suited to people who are incapable of any interest in psychology. But the fine artists must keep the policeman out of his studies of sex and studies of crime. It is by clinging nervously to the policeman that most of the pseudo sex plays convince me that the writers have either never had any serious personal experience of their ostensible subject, or else have never conceived it possible that the stage door present the phenomena of sex as they appear in nature.

THE LIMITS OF STAGE PRESENTATION.

But the stage presents much more shocking phenomena than those of sex. There is, of course, a sense in which you cannot present sex on the stage, just as you cannot present murder. Macbeth must no more really kill Duncan than he must himself be really slain by Macduff. But the feelings of a murderer can be expressed in a certain artistic convention; and a carefully prearranged sword exercise can be gone through with sufficient pretence of earnestness to be accepted by the willing imaginations of the younger spectators as a desperate combat.

The tragedy of love has been presented on the stage in the same way. In Tristan and Isolde, the curtain does not, as in Romeo and Juliet, rise with the lark: the whole night of love is played before the spectators. The lovers do not discuss marriage in an elegantly sentimental way: they utter the visions and feelings that come to lovers at the supreme moments of their love, totally forgetting that there are such things in the world as husbands and lawyers and duelling codes and theories of sin and notions of propriety and all the other irrelevancies which provide hackneyed and bloodless material for our so-called plays of passion.

PRUDERIES OF THE FRENCH STAGE.

To all stage presentations there are limits. If Macduff were to stab Macbeth, the spectacle would be intolerable; and even the pretence which we allow on our stage is ridiculously destructive to the illusion of the scene. Yet pugilists and gladiators will actually fight and kill in public without sham, even as a spectacle for money. But no sober couple of lovers of any delicacy could endure to be watched. We in

England, accustomed to consider the French stage much more licentious than the British, are always surprised and puzzled when we learn, as we may do any day if we come within reach of such information, that French actors are often scandalized by what they consider the indecency of the English stage, and that French actresses who desire a greater license in appealing to the sexual instincts than the French stage allows them, learn and establish themselves on the English stage. The German and Russian stages are in the same relation to the French and perhaps more or less all the Latin stages. The reason is that, partly from a want of respect for the theatre, partly from a sort of respect for art in general which moves them to accord moral privileges to artists, partly from the very objectionable tradition that the realm of art is Alsatia and the contemplation of works of art a holiday from the burden of virtue, partly because French prudery does not attach itself to the same points of behavior as British prudery, and has a different code of the mentionable and the unmentionable, and for many other reasons the French tolerate plays which are never performed in England until they have been spoiled by a process of bowdlerization; yet French taste is more fastidious than ours as to the exhibition and treatment on the stage of the physical incidents of sex. On the French stage a kiss is as obvious a convention as the thrust under the arm by which Macduff runs Macbeth through. It is even a purposely unconvincing convention: the actors rather insisting that it shall be impossible for any spectator to mistake a stage kiss for a real one. In England, on the contrary, realism is carried to the point at which nobody except the two performers can perceive that the caress is not genuine. And here the English stage is certainly in the right; for whatever question there arises as to what incidents are proper for representation on the stage or not, my experience as a playgoer leaves me in no doubt that once it is decided to represent an incident, it will be offensive, no matter whether it be a prayer or a kiss, unless it is presented with a convincing appearance of sincerity.

OUR DISILLUSIVE SCENERY.

For example, the main objection to the use of illusive scenery (in most modern plays scenery is not illusive; everything visible is as real as in your drawing room at home) is that it is unconvincing; whilst the imaginary scenery with which the audience provides a platform or tribune like the Elizabethan stage or the Greek stage used by Sophocles, is quite convincing. In fact, the more scenery you have the less illusion you produce. The wise playwright, when he cannot get absolute reality of presentation, goes to the other extreme, and aims at atmosphere and suggestion of mood rather than at direct simulative illusion. The theatre, as I first knew it, was a place of wings and flats which destroyed both atmosphere and illusion. This was tolerated, and even intensely enjoyed, but not in the least because nothing better was possible; for all the devices employed in the productions of Mr. Granville Barker or Max Reinhardt or the Moscow Art Theatre were equally available for Colley Cibber and Garrick, except the intensity of our artificial light. When Garrick played Richard II in slashed trunk hose and plumes, it was not because he believed that the Plantagenets dressed like that, or because the costumes could not have made him a XV century dress as easily as a nondescript combination of the state robes of George III with such scraps of older fashions as seemed to playgoers for some reason to be romantic. The charm of the theatre in those days was its makebelieve. It has that charm still, not only for the amateurs, who are happiest when they are most unnatural and impossible and absurd, but for audiences as well. I have seen performances of my own plays which were to me far wilder burlesques than Sheridan's Critic or Buckingham's Rehearsal; yet they have produced sincere laughter and tears such as the most finished metropolitan productions have failed to elicit. Fielding was entirely right when he represented Partridge as enjoying intensely the performance of the king in Hamlet because anybody could see that the king was an actor, and resenting Garrick's Hamlet because it might have been a real man. Yet we have only to look at the portraits of Garrick to see that his performances would nowadays seem almost as extravagantly stagey as his costumes. In our day Calve's intensely real Carmen never pleased the mob as much as the obvious fancy ball masquerading of suburban young ladies in the same character.

HOLDING THE MIRROR UP TO NATURE.

Theatrical art begins as the holding up to Nature of a distorting mirror. In this phase it pleases people who are childish enough to believe that they can see what they look like and what they are when they look at a true mirror. Naturally they think that a true mirror can teach them nothing. Only by giving them back some monstrous image can the mirror amuse them or terrify them. It is not until they grow up to the point at which they learn that they know very little about themselves, and that they do not see themselves in a true mirror as other people see them, that they become consumed with curiosity as to what they really are like, and begin to demand that the stage shall be a mirror of such accuracy and intensity of illumination that they shall be able to get glimpses of their real selves in it, and also learn a little how they appear to other people.

For audiences of this highly developed class, sex can no longer be ignored or conventionalized or distorted by the playwright who makes the mirror. The old sentimental extravagances and the old grossnesses are of no further use to him. Don Giovanni and Zerlina are not gross: Tristan and Isolde are not extravagant or sentimental. They say and do nothing that you cannot bear to hear and see; and yet they give you, the one pair briefly and slightly, and the other fully and deeply, what passes in the minds of lovers. The love depicted may be that of a philosophic adventurer tempting an ignorant country girl, or of a tragically serious poet entangled with a woman of noble capacity in a passion which has become for them the reality of the whole universe. No matter: the thing is dramatized and dramatized directly, not talked about as something that happened before the curtain rose, or that will happen after it falls.

FARCICAL COMEDY SHIRKING ITS SUBJECT.

Now if all this can be done in the key of tragedy and philosophic comedy, it can, I have always contended, be done in the key of farcical comedy; and Overruled is a trifling experiment in that manner. Conventional farcical comedies are always finally tedious because the heart of them, the inevitable conjugal infidelity, is always evaded. Even its consequences are evaded. Mr. Granville Barker has pointed out rightly that if the third acts of our farcical comedies dared to describe the consequences that would follow from the first and second in real life, they would end as squalid tragedies; and in my opinion they would be greatly improved thereby even as entertainments; for I have never seen a three-act farcical comedy without being bored and tired by the third act, and observing that the rest of the audience were in the same condition, though they were not vigilantly introspective enough to find that out, and were apt to blame one another, especially the husbands and wives, for their crossness. But it is happily by no means true that conjugal infidelities always produce tragic consequences, or that they need produce even the unhappiness which they often do produce. Besides, the more momentous the consequences, the more interesting become the impulses and imaginations and reasonings, if any, of the people who disregard them. If I had an opportunity of conversing with the ghost of an executed murderer, I have no doubt he would begin to tell me eagerly about his trial, with the names of the distinguished ladies and gentlemen who honored him with their presence on that occasion, and then about his execution. All of which would bore me exceedingly. I should say, "My dear sir: such manufactured ceremonies do not interest me in the least. I know how a man is tried, and how he is hanged. I should have had you killed in a much less disgusting, hypocritical, and unfriendly manner if the matter had been in my hands. What I want to know about is the murder. How did you feel when you committed it? Why did you do it? What did you say to yourself about it? If, like most murderers, you had not been hanged, would you have committed other murders? Did you really dislike the victim, or did you want his money, or did you murder a person whom you did not dislike, and from whose death you had nothing to gain, merely for the sake of murdering? If so, can you describe the charm to me? Does it come upon you periodically; or is it chronic? Has curiosity anything to do with it?" I would ply him with all manner of questions to find out what murder is really like; and I should not be satisfied until I had realized that I, too, might commit a murder, or else that there is some specific quality present in a murderer and lacking in me. And, if so, what that quality is.

In just the same way, I want the unfaithful husband or the unfaithful wife in a farcical comedy not to bother me with their divorce cases or the stratagems they employ to avoid a divorce case, but to tell me how and why married couples are unfaithful. I don't want to hear the lies they tell one another to conceal what they have done, but the truths they tell one another when they have to face what they have done without concealment or excuse. No doubt prudent and considerate people conceal such adventures, when they can, from those who are most likely to be wounded by them; but it is not to be presumed that, when found out, they necessarily disgrace themselves by irritating lies and transparent subterfuges.

My playlet, which I offer as a model to all future writers of farcical comedy, may now, I hope, be read without shock. I may just add that Mr.

Sibthorpe Juno's view that morality demands, not that we should behave morally (an impossibility to our sinful nature) but that we shall not attempt to defend our immoralities, is a standard view in England, and was advanced in all seriousness by an earnest and distinguished British moralist shortly after the first performance of Overruled. My objection to that aspect of the doctrine of original sin is that no necessary and inevitable operation of human nature can reasonably be regarded as sinful at all, and that a morality which assumes the contrary is an absurd morality, and can be kept in countenance only by hypocrisy. When people were ashamed of sanitary problems, and refused to face them, leaving them to solve themselves clandestinely in dirt and secrecy, the solution arrived at was the Black Death. A similar policy as to sex problems has solved itself by an even worse plague than the Black Death; and the remedy for that is not Salvarsan, but sound moral hygiene, the first foundation of which is the discontinuance of our habit of telling not only the comparatively harmless lies that we know we ought not to tell, but the ruinous lies that we foolishly think we ought to tell.

OVERRULED.

A lady and gentleman are sitting together on a chesterfield in a retired corner of the lounge of a seaside hotel. It is a summer night: the French window behind them stands open. The terrace without overlooks a moonlit harbor. The lounge is dark. The chesterfield, upholstered in silver grey, and the two figures on it in evening dress, catch the light from an arc lamp somewhere; but the walls, covered with a dark green paper, are in gloom. There are two stray chairs, one on each side. On the gentleman's right, behind him up near the window, is an unused fireplace. Opposite it on the lady's left is a door. The gentleman is on the lady's right.

The lady is very attractive, with a musical voice and soft appealing manners. She is young: that is, one feels sure that she is under thirty-five and over twenty-four. The gentleman does not look much older. He is rather handsome, and has ventured as far in the direction of poetic dandyism in the arrangement of his hair as any man who is not a professional artist can afford to in England. He is obviously very much in love with the lady, and is, in fact, yielding to an irresistible impulse to throw his arms around her.

THE LADY. Don't--oh don't be horrid. Please, Mr. Lunn [she rises from the lounge and retreats behind it]! Promise me you won't be horrid.

GREGORY LUNN. I'm not being horrid, Mrs. Juno. I'm not going to be horrid. I love you: that's all. I'm extraordinarily happy.

MRS. JUNO. You will really be good?

GREGORY. I'll be whatever you wish me to be. I tell you I love you. I love loving you. I don't want to be tired and sorry, as I should be if I were to be horrid. I don't want you to be tired and sorry. Do come and sit down again.

MRS. JUNO [coming back to her seat]. You're sure you don't want anything you oughtn't to?

GREGORY. Quite sure. I only want you [she recoils]. Don't be alarmed. I like wanting you. As long as I have a want, I have a reason for living. Satisfaction is death.

MRS. JUNO. Yes; but the impulse to commit suicide is sometimes irresistible.

GREGORY. Not with you.

MRS. JUNO. What!

GREGORY. Oh, it sounds uncomplimentary; but it isn't really. Do you know why half the couples who find themselves situated as we are now behave horridly?

MRS. JUNO. Because they can't help it if they let things go too far.

GREGORY. Not a bit of it. It's because they have nothing else to do, and no other way of entertaining each other. You don't know what it is to be alone with a woman who has little beauty and less conversation. What is a man to do? She can't talk interestingly; and if he talks that way himself she doesn't understand him. He can't look at her: if he does, he only finds out that she isn't beautiful. Before the end of five minutes they are both hideously bored. There's only one thing that can save the situation; and that's what you call being horrid. With a beautiful, witty, kind woman, there's no time for such follies. It's so delightful to look at her, to listen to her voice, to hear all she has to say, that nothing else happens. That is why the woman who is supposed to have a thousand lovers seldom has one; whilst the stupid, graceless animals of women have dozens.

MRS. JUNO. I wonder! It's quite true that when one feels in danger one talks like mad to stave it off, even when one doesn't quite want to stave it off.

GREGORY. One never does quite want to stave it off. Danger is delicious. But death isn't. We court the danger; but the real delight is in escaping, after all.

MRS. JUNO. I don't think we'll talk about it any more. Danger is all very well when you do escape; but sometimes one doesn't. I tell you frankly I don't feel as safe as you do--if you really do.

GREGORY. But surely you can do as you please without injuring anyone, Mrs. Juno. That is the whole secret of your extraordinary charm for me.

MRS. JUNO. I don't understand.

GREGORY. Well, I hardly know how to begin to explain. But the root of the matter is that I am what people call a good man.

MRS. JUNO. I thought so until you began making love to me.

GREGORY. But you knew I loved you all along.

MRS. JUNO. Yes, of course; but I depended on you not to tell me so; because I thought you were good. Your blurting it out spoilt it. And it was wicked besides.

GREGORY. Not at all. You see, it's a great many years since I've been able to allow myself to fall in love. I know lots of charming women; but the worst of it is, they're all married. Women don't become charming, to my taste, until they're fully developed; and by that time, if they're really nice, they're snapped up and married. And then, because I am a good man, I have to place a limit to my regard for them. I may be fortunate enough to gain friendship and even very warm affection from them; but my loyalty to their husbands and their hearths and their happiness obliges me to draw a line and not overstep it. Of course I value such affectionate regard very highly indeed. I am surrounded with women who are most dear to me. But every one of them has a post sticking up, if I may put it that way, with the inscription

Trespassers Will Be Prosecuted. How we all loathe that notice! In every
lovely garden, in every dell full of primroses, on every fair hillside,
we meet that confounded board; and there is always a gamekeeper round
the corner. But what is that to the horror of meeting it on every
beautiful woman, and knowing that there is a husband round the corner?
I have had this accursed board standing between me and every dear and
desirable woman until I thought I had lost the power of letting myself
fall really and wholeheartedly in love.

MRS. JUNO. Wasn't there a widow?

GREGORY. No. Widows are extraordinarily scarce in modern society.
Husbands live longer than they used to; and even when they do die,
their widows have a string of names down for their next.

MRS. JUNO. Well, what about the young girls?

GREGORY. Oh, who cares for young girls? They're sympathetic. They're
beginners. They don't attract me. I'm afraid of them.

MRS. JUNO. That's the correct thing to say to a woman of my age. But it
doesn't explain why you seem to have put your scruples in your pocket
when you met me.

GREGORY. Surely that's quite clear. I--

MRS. JUNO. No: please don't explain. I don't want to know. I take your
word for it. Besides, it doesn't matter now. Our voyage is over; and
to-morrow I start for the north to my poor father's place.

GREGORY [surprised]. Your poor father! I thought he was alive.

MRS. JUNO. So he is. What made you think he wasn't?

GREGORY. You said your POOR father.

MRS. JUNO. Oh, that's a trick of mine. Rather a silly trick, I Suppose;
but there's something pathetic to me about men: I find myself calling
them poor So-and-So when there's nothing whatever the matter with them.

GREGORY [who has listened in growing alarm]. But--I--is?-- wa--? Oh,
Lord!

MRS. JUNO. What's the matter?

GREGORY. Nothing.

MRS. JUNO. Nothing! [Rising anxiously]. Nonsense: you're ill.

GREGORY. No. It was something about your late husband--

MRS. JUNO. My LATE husband! What do you mean? [clutching him,
horror-stricken]. Don't tell me he's dead.

GREGORY [rising, equally appalled]. Don't tell me he's alive.

MRS. JUNO. Oh, don't frighten me like this. Of course he's
alive--unless you've heard anything.

GREGORY. The first day we met--on the boat--you spoke to me of your
poor dear husband.

MRS. JUNO [releasing him, quite reassured]. Is that all?

GREGORY. Well, afterwards you called him poor Tops. Always poor Tops,
Our poor dear Tops. What could I think?

MRS. JUNO [sitting down again]. I wish you hadn't given me such a shock about him; for I haven't been treating him at all well. Neither have you.

GREGORY [relapsing into his seat, overwhelmed]. And you mean to tell me you're not a widow!

MRS. JUNO. Gracious, no! I'm not in black.

GREGORY. Then I have been behaving like a blackguard. I have broken my promise to my mother. I shall never have an easy conscience again.

MRS. JUNO. I'm sorry. I thought you knew.

GREGORY. You thought I was a libertine?

MRS. JUNO. No: of course I shouldn't have spoken to you if I had thought that. I thought you liked me, but that you knew, and would be good.

GREGORY [stretching his hands towards her breast]. I thought the burden of being good had fallen from my soul at last. I saw nothing there but a bosom to rest on: the bosom of a lovely woman of whom I could dream without guilt. What do I see now?

MRS. JUNO. Just what you saw before.

GREGORY [despairingly]. No, no.

MRS. JUNO. What else?

GREGORY. Trespassers Will Be Prosecuted: Trespassers Will Be Prosecuted.

MRS. JUNO. They won't if they hold their tongues. Don't be such a coward. My husband won't eat you.

GREGORY. I'm not afraid of your husband. I'm afraid of my conscience.

MRS. JUNO [losing patience]. Well! I don't consider myself at all a badly behaved woman; for nothing has passed between us that was not perfectly nice and friendly; but really! to hear a grown-up man talking about promises to his mother!

GREGORY [interrupting her]. Yes, Yes: I know all about that. It's not romantic: it's not Don Juan: it's not advanced; but we feel it all the same. It's far deeper in our blood and bones than all the romantic stuff. My father got into a scandal once: that was why my mother made me promise never to make love to a married woman. And now I've done it I can't feel honest. Don't pretend to despise me or laugh at me. You feel it too. You said just now that your own conscience was uneasy when you thought of your husband. What must it be when you think of my wife?

MRS. JUNO [rising aghast]. Your wife!!! You don't dare sit there and tell me coolly that you're a married man!

GREGORY. I never led you to believe I was unmarried.

MRS. JUNO. Oh! You never gave me the faintest hint that you had a wife.

GREGORY. I did indeed. I discussed things with you that only married people really understand.

MRS. JUNO. Oh!!

GREGORY. I thought it the most delicate way of letting you know.

MRS. JUNO. Well, you ARE a daisy, I must say. I suppose that's vulgar; but really! really!! You and your goodness! However, now we've found one another out there's only one thing to be done. Will you please go?

GREGORY [rising slowly]. I OUGHT to go.

MRS. JUNO. Well, go.

GREGORY. Yes. Er--[he tries to go]. I--I somehow can't. [He sits down again helplessly]. My conscience is active: my will is paralyzed. This is really dreadful. Would you mind ringing the bell and asking them to throw me out? You ought to, you know.

MRS. JUNO. What! make a scandal in the face of the whole hotel! Certainly not. Don't be a fool.

GREGORY. Yes; but I can't go.

MRS. JUNO. Then I can. Goodbye.

GREGORY [clinging to her hand]. Can you really?

MRS. JUNO. Of course I--[she wavers]. Oh, dear! [They contemplate one another helplessly]. I can't. [She sinks on the lounge, hand in hand with him].

GREGORY. For heaven's sake pull yourself together. It's a question of self-control.

MRS. JUNO [dragging her hand away and retreating to the end of the chesterfield]. No: it's a question of distance. Self-control is all very well two or three yards off, or on a ship, with everybody looking on. Don't come any nearer.

GREGORY. This is a ghastly business. I want to go away; and I can't.

MRS. JUNO. I think you ought to go [he makes an effort; and she adds quickly] but if you try I shall grab you round the neck and disgrace myself. I implore you to sit still and be nice.

GREGORY. I implore you to run away. I believe I can trust myself to let you go for your own sake. But it will break my heart.

MRS. JUNO. I don't want to break your heart. I can't bear to think of your sitting here alone. I can't bear to think of sitting alone myself somewhere else. It's so senseless--so ridiculous--when we might be so happy. I don't want to be wicked, or coarse. But I like you very much; and I do want to be affectionate and human.

GREGORY. I ought to draw a line.

MRS. JUNO. So you shall, dear. Tell me: do you really like me? I don't mean LOVE me: you might love the housemaid--

GREGORY [vehemently]. No!

MRS. JUNO. Oh, yes you might; and what does that matter, anyhow? Are you really fond of me? Are we friends--comrades? Would you be sorry if I died?

GREGORY [shrinking]. Oh, don't.

MRS. JUNO. Or was it the usual aimless man's lark: a mere shipboard flirtation?

GREGORY. Oh, no, no: nothing half so bad, so vulgar, so wrong. I assure you I only meant to be agreeable. It grew on me before I noticed it.

MRS. JUNO. And you were glad to let it grow?

GREGORY. I let it grow because the board was not up.

MRS. JUNO. Bother the board! I am just as fond of Sibthorpe as--

GREGORY. Sibthorpe!

MRS. JUNO. Sibthorpe is my husband's Christian name. I oughtn't to call him Tops to you now.

GREGORY [chuckling]. It sounded like something to drink. But I have no right to laugh at him. My Christian name is Gregory, which sounds like a powder.

MRS. JUNO [chilled]. That is so like a man! I offer you my heart's warmest friendliest feeling; and you think of nothing but a silly joke. A quip like that makes you forget me.

GREGORY. Forget you! Oh, if I only could!

MRS. JUNO. If you could, would you?

GREGORY [burying his shamed face in his hands]. No: I'd die first. Oh, I hate myself.

MRS. JUNO. I glory in myself. It's so jolly to be reckless. CAN a man be reckless, I wonder.

GREGORY [straightening himself desperately]. No. I'm not reckless. I know what I'm doing: my conscience is awake. Oh, where is the intoxication of love? the delirium? the madness that makes a man think the world well lost for the woman he adores? I don't think anything of the sort: I see that it's not worth it: I know that it's wrong: I have never in my life been cooler, more businesslike.

MRS. JUNO. [opening her arms to him] But you can't resist me.

GREGORY. I must. I ought [throwing himself into her arms]. Oh, my darling, my treasure, we shall be sorry for this.

MRS. JUNO. We can forgive ourselves. Could we forgive ourselves if we let this moment slip?

GREGORY. I protest to the last. I'm against this. I have been pushed over a precipice. I'm innocent. This wild joy, this exquisite tenderness, this ascent into heaven can thrill me to the uttermost fibre of my heart [with a gesture of ecstasy she hides her face on his shoulder]; but it can't subdue my mind or corrupt my conscience, which still shouts to the skies that I'm not a willing party to this outrageous conduct. I repudiate the bliss with which you are filling me.

MRS. JUNO. Never mind your conscience. Tell me how happy you are.

GREGORY. No, I recall you to your duty. But oh, I will give you my life with both hands if you can tell me that you feel for me one millionth part of what I feel for you now.

MRS. JUNO. Oh, yes, yes. Be satisfied with that. Ask for no more. Let me go.

GREGORY. I can't. I have no will. Something stronger than either of us is in command here. Nothing on earth or in heaven can part us now. You know that, don't you?

MRS. JUNO. Oh, don't make me say it. Of course I know. Nothing--not life nor death nor shame nor anything can part us.

A MATTER-OF-FACT MALE VOICE IN THE CORRIDOR. All right. This must be it.

The two recover with a violent start; release one another; and spring back to opposite sides of the lounge.

GREGORY. That did it.

MRS. JUNO [in a thrilling whisper] Sh--sh--sh! That was my husband's voice.

GREGORY. Impossible: it's only our guilty fancy.

A WOMAN'S VOICE. This is the way to the lounge. I know it.

GREGORY. Great Heaven! we're both mad. That's my wife's voice.

MRS. JUNO. Ridiculous! Oh! we're dreaming it all. We [the door opens; and Sibthorpe Juno appears in the roseate glow of the corridor (which happens to be papered in pink) with Mrs. Lunn, like Tannhauser in the hill of Venus. He is a fussily energetic little man, who gives himself an air of gallantry by greasing the points of his moustaches and dressing very carefully. She is a tall, imposing, handsome, languid woman, with flashing dark eyes and long lashes. They make for the chesterfield, not noticing the two palpitating figures blotted against the walls in the gloom on either side. The figures flit away noiselessly through the window and disappear].

JUNO [officiously] Ah: here we are. [He leads the way to the sofa]. Sit down: I'm sure you're tired. [She sits]. That's right. [He sits beside her on her left]. Hullo! [he rises] this sofa's quite warm.

MRS. LUNN [bored] Is it? I don't notice it. I expect the sun's been on it.

JUNO. I felt it quite distinctly: I'm more thinly clad than you. [He sits down again, and proceeds, with a sigh of satisfaction]. What a relief to get off the ship and have a private room! That's the worst of a ship. You're under observation all the time.

MRS. LUNN. But why not?

JUNO. Well, of course there's no reason: at least I suppose not. But, you know, part of the romance of a journey is that a man keeps imagining that something might happen; and he can't do that if there are a lot of people about and it simply can't happen.

MRS. LUNN. Mr. Juno: romance is all very well on board ship; but when your foot touches the soil of England there's an end of it.

JUNO. No: believe me, that's a foreigner's mistake: we are the most romantic people in the world, we English. Why, my very presence here is a romance.

MRS. LUNN [faintly ironical] Indeed?

JUNO. Yes. You've guessed, of course, that I'm a married man.

MRS. LUNN. Oh, that's all right. I'm a married woman.

JUNO. Thank Heaven for that! To my English mind, passion is not real passion without guilt. I am a red-blooded man, Mrs. Lunn: I can't help it. The tragedy of my life is that I married, when quite young, a woman whom I couldn't help being very fond of. I longed for a guilty passion--for the real thing--the wicked thing; and yet I couldn't care twopence for any other woman when my wife was about. Year after year went by: I felt my youth slipping away without ever having had a romance in my life; for marriage is all very well; but it isn't romance. There's nothing wrong in it, you see.

MRS. LUNN. Poor man! How you must have suffered!

JUNO. No: that was what was so tame about it. I wanted to suffer. You get so sick of being happily married. It's always the happy marriages that break up. At last my wife and I agreed that we ought to take a holiday.

MRS. LUNN. Hadn't you holidays every year?

JUNO. Oh, the seaside and so on! That's not what we meant. We meant a holiday from one another.

MRS. LUNN. How very odd!

JUNO. She said it was an excellent idea; that domestic felicity was making us perfectly idiotic; that she wanted a holiday, too. So we agreed to go round the world in opposite directions. I started for Suez on the day she sailed for New York.

MRS. LUNN [suddenly becoming attentive] That's precisely what Gregory and I did. Now I wonder did he want a holiday from me! What he said was that he wanted the delight of meeting me after a long absence.

JUNO. Could anything be more romantic than that? Would anyone else than an Englishman have thought of it? I daresay my temperament seems tame to your boiling southern blood--

MRS. LUNN. My what!

JUNO. Your southern blood. Don't you remember how you told me, that night in the saloon when I sang "Farewell and adieu to you dear Spanish ladies," that you were by birth a lady of Spain? Your splendid Andalusian beauty speaks for itself.

MRS. LUNN. Stuff! I was born in Gibraltar. My father was Captain Jenkins. In the artillery.

JUNO [ardently] It is climate and not race that determines the temperament. The fiery sun of Spain blazed on your cradle; and it rocked to the roar of British cannon.

MRS. LUNN. What eloquence! It reminds me of my husband when he was in love before we were married. Are you in love?

JUNO. Yes; and with the same woman.

MRS. LUNN. Well, of course, I didn't suppose you were in love with two women.

JUNO. I don't think you quite understand. I meant that I am in love with you.

MRS. LUNN [relapsing into deepest boredom] Oh, that! Men do fall in love with me. They all seem to think me a creature with volcanic passions: I'm sure I don't know why; for all the volcanic women I know are plain little creatures with sandy hair. I don't consider human volcanoes respectable. And I'm so tired of the subject! Our house is always full of women who are in love with my husband and men who are in love with me. We encourage it because it's pleasant to have company.

JUNO. And is your husband as insensible as yourself?

MRS. LUNN. Oh, Gregory's not insensible: very far from it; but I am the only woman in the world for him.

JUNO. But you? Are you really as insensible as you say you are?

MRS. LUNN. I never said anything of the kind. I'm not at all insensible by nature; but (I don't know whether you've noticed it) I am what people call rather a fine figure of a woman.

JUNO [passionately] Noticed it! Oh, Mrs. Lunn! Have I been able to notice anything else since we met?

MRS. LUNN. There you go, like all the rest of them! I ask you, how do you expect a woman to keep up what you call her sensibility when this sort of thing has happened to her about three times a week ever since she was seventeen? It used to upset me and terrify me at first. Then I got rather a taste for it. It came to a climax with Gregory: that was why I married him. Then it became a mild lark, hardly worth the trouble. After that I found it valuable once or twice as a spinal tonic when I was run down; but now it's an unmitigated bore. I don't mind your declaration: I daresay it gives you a certain pleasure to make it. I quite understand that you adore me; but (if you don't mind) I'd rather you didn't keep on saying so.

JUNO. Is there then no hope for me?

MRS. LUNN. Oh, yes. Gregory has an idea that married women keep lists of the men they'll marry if they become widows. I'll put your name down, if that will satisfy you.

JUNO. Is the list a long one?

MRS. LUNN. Do you mean the real list? Not the one I show to Gregory: there are hundreds of names on that; but the little private list that he'd better not see?

JUNO. Oh, will you really put me on that? Say you will.

MRS. LUNN. Well, perhaps I will. [He kisses her hand]. Now don't begin abusing the privilege.

JUNO. May I call you by your Christian name?

MRS. LUNN. No: it's too long. You can't go about calling a woman Seraphita.

JUNO [ecstatically] Seraphita!

MRS. LUNN. I used to be called Sally at home; but when I married a man named Lunn, of course that became ridiculous. That's my one little pet joke. Call me Mrs. Lunn for short. And change the subject, or I shall go to sleep.

JUNO. I can't change the subject. For me there is no other subject. Why else have you put me on your list?

MRS. LUNN. Because you're a solicitor. Gregory's a solicitor. I'm accustomed to my husband being a solicitor and telling me things he oughtn't to tell anybody.

JUNO [ruefully] Is that all? Oh, I can't believe that the voice of love has ever thoroughly awakened you.

MRS. LUNN. No: it sends me to sleep. [Juno appeals against this by an amorous demonstration]. It's no use, Mr. Juno: I'm hopelessly respectable: the Jenkinses always were. Don't you realize that unless most women were like that, the world couldn't go on as it does?

JUNO [darkly] You think it goes on respectably; but I can tell you as a solicitor--

MRS. LUNN. Stuff! of course all the disreputable people who get into trouble go to you, just as all the sick people go to the doctors; but most people never go to a solicitor.

JUNO [rising, with a growing sense of injury] Look here, Mrs. Lunn: do you think a man's heart is a potato? or a turnip? or a ball of knitting wool? that you can throw it away like this?

MRS. LUNN. I don't throw away balls of knitting wool. A man's heart seems to me much like a sponge: it sops up dirty water as well as clean.

JUNO. I have never been treated like this in my life. Here am I, a married man, with a most attractive wife: a wife I adore, and who adores me, and has never as much as looked at any other man since we were married. I come and throw all this at your feet. I! I, a solicitor! braving the risk of your husband putting me into the divorce court and making me a beggar and an outcast! I do this for your sake. And you go on as if I were making no sacrifice: as if I had told you it's a fine evening, or asked you to have a cup of tea. It's not human. It's not right. Love has its rights as well as respectability [he sits down again, aloof and sulky].

MRS. LUNN. Nonsense! Here, here's a flower [she gives him one]. Go and dream over it until you feel hungry. Nothing brings people to their senses like hunger.

JUNO [contemplating the flower without rapture] What good's this?

MRS. LUNN [snatching it from him] Oh! you don't love me a bit.

JUNO. Yes I do. Or at least I did. But I'm an Englishman; and I think you ought to respect the conventions of English life.

MRS. LUNN. But I am respecting them; and you're not.

JUNO. Pardon me. I may be doing wrong; but I'm doing it in a proper and customary manner. You may be doing right; but you're doing it in an unusual and questionable manner. I am not prepared to put up with that. I can stand being badly treated: I'm no baby, and can take care of myself with anybody. And of course I can stand being well treated. But the thing I can't stand is being unexpectedly treated, It's outside my scheme of life. So come now! you've got to behave naturally and straightforwardly with me. You can leave husband and child, home, friends, and country, for my sake, and come with me to some southern isle--or say South America--where we can be all in all to one another. Or you can tell your husband and let him jolly well punch my head if he can. But I'm damned if I'm going to stand any eccentricity. It's not respectable.

GREGORY [coming in from the terrace and advancing with dignity to his wife's end of the chesterfield]. Will you have the goodness, sir, in addressing this lady, to keep your temper and refrain from using profane language?

MRS. LUNN [rising, delighted] Gregory! Darling [she enfolds him in a copious embrace]!

JUNO [rising] You make love to another man to my face!

MRS. LUNN. Why, he's my husband.

JUNO. That takes away the last rag of excuse for such conduct. A nice world it would be if married people were to carry on their endearments before everybody!

GREGORY. This is ridiculous. What the devil business is it of yours what passes between my wife and myself? You're not her husband, are you?

JUNO. Not at present; but I'm on the list. I'm her prospective husband: you're only her actual one. I'm the anticipation: you're the disappointment.

MRS. LUNN. Oh, my Gregory is not a disappointment. [Fondly] Are you, dear?

GREGORY. You just wait, my pet. I'll settle this chap for you. [He disengages himself from her embrace, and faces Juno. She sits down placidly]. You call me a disappointment, do you? Well, I suppose every husband's a disappointment. What about yourself? Don't try to look like an unmarried man. I happen to know the lady you disappointed. I travelled in the same ship with her; and--

JUNO. And you fell in love with her.

GREGORY [taken aback] Who told you that?

JUNO. Aha! you confess it. Well, if you want to know, nobody told me. Everybody falls in love with my wife.

GREGORY. And do you fall in love with everybody's wife?

JUNO. Certainly not. Only with yours.

MRS. LUNN. But what's the good of saying that, Mr. Juno? I'm married to him; and there's an end of it.

JUNO. Not at all. You can get a divorce.

MRS. LUNN. What for?

JUNO. For his misconduct with my wife.

GREGORY [deeply indignant] How dare you, sir, asperse the character of that sweet lady? a lady whom I have taken under my protection.

JUNO. Protection!

MRS. JUNO [returning hastily] Really you must be more careful what you say about me, Mr. Lunn.

JUNO. My precious! [He embraces her]. Pardon this betrayal of my feeling; but I've not seen my wife for several weeks; and she is very dear to me.

GREGORY. I call this cheek. Who is making love to his own wife before people now, pray?

MRS. LUNN. Won't you introduce me to your wife, Mr. Juno?

MRS. JUNO. How do you do? [They shake hands; and Mrs. Juno sits down beside Mrs. Lunn, on her left].

MRS. LUNN. I'm so glad to find you do credit to Gregory's taste. I'm naturally rather particular about the women he falls in love with.

JUNO [sternly] This is no way to take your husband's unfaithfulness. [To Lunn] You ought to teach your wife better. Where's her feelings? It's scandalous.

GREGORY. What about your own conduct, pray?

JUNO. I don't defend it; and there's an end of the matter.

GREGORY. Well, upon my soul! What difference does your not defending it make?

JUNO. A fundamental difference. To serious people I may appear wicked. I don't defend myself: I am wicked, though not bad at heart. To thoughtless people I may even appear comic. Well, laugh at me: I have given myself away. But Mrs. Lunn seems to have no opinion at all about me. She doesn't seem to know whether I'm wicked or comic. She doesn't seem to care. She has no more sense. I say it's not right. I repeat, I have sinned; and I'm prepared to suffer.

MRS. JUNO. Have you really sinned, Tops?

MRS. LUNN [blandly] I don't remember your sinning. I have a shocking bad memory for trifles; but I think I should remember that--if you mean me.

JUNO [raging] Trifles! I have fallen in love with a monster.

GREGORY. Don't you dare call my wife a monster.

MRS. JUNO [rising quickly and coming between them]. Please don't lose your temper, Mr. Lunn: I won't have my Tops bullied.

GREGORY. Well, then, let him not brag about sinning with my wife. [He turns impulsively to his wife; makes her rise; and takes her proudly on his arm]. What pretension has he to any such honor?

JUNO. I sinned in intention. [Mrs. Juno abandons him and resumes her seat, chilled]. I'm as guilty as if I had actually sinned. And I insist on being treated as a sinner, and not walked over as if I'd done nothing, by your wife or any other man.

MRS. LUNN. Tush! [She sits down again contemptuously].

JUNO [furious] I won't be belittled.

MRS. LUNN [to Mrs. Juno] I hope you'll come and stay with us now that you and Gregory are such friends, Mrs. Juno.

JUNO. This insane magnanimity--

MRS. LUNN. Don't you think you've said enough, Mr. Juno? This is a matter for two women to settle. Won't you take a stroll on the beach with my Gregory while we talk it over. Gregory is a splendid listener.

JUNO. I don't think any good can come of a conversation between Mr. Lunn and myself. We can hardly be expected to improve one another's morals. [He passes behind the chesterfield to Mrs. Lunn's end; seizes a chair; deliberately pushes it between Gregory and Mrs. Lunn; and sits down with folded arms, resolved not to budge].

GREGORY. Oh! Indeed! Oh, all right. If you come to that--[he crosses to Mrs. Juno; plants a chair by her side; and sits down with equal determination].

JUNO. Now we are both equally guilty.

GREGORY. Pardon me. I'm not guilty.

JUNO. In intention. Don't quibble. You were guilty in intention, as I was.

GREGORY. No. I should rather describe myself guilty in fact, but not in intention.

JUNO   { rising and   } What!
MRS. JUNO   { exclaiming } No, really--
MRS. LUNN   { simultaneously } Gregory!

GREGORY. Yes: I maintain that I am responsible for my intentions only, and not for reflex actions over which I have no control. [Mrs. Juno sits down, ashamed]. I promised my mother that I would never tell a lie, and that I would never make love to a married woman. I never have told a lie--

MRS. LUNN [remonstrating] Gregory! [She sits down again].

GREGORY. I say never. On many occasions I have resorted to prevarication; but on great occasions I have always told the truth. I regard this as a great occasion; and I won't be intimidated into breaking my promise. I solemnly declare that I did not know until this evening that Mrs. Juno was married. She will bear me out when I say that from that moment my intentions were strictly and resolutely honorable; though my conduct, which I could not control and am therefore not responsible for, was disgraceful--or would have been had this gentleman not walked in and begun making love to my wife under my very nose.

JUNO [flinging himself back into his chair] Well, I like this!

MRS. LUNN. Really, darling, there's no use in the pot calling the kettle black.

GREGORY. When you say darling, may I ask which of us you are addressing?

MRS. LUNN. I really don't know. I'm getting hopelessly confused.

JUNO. Why don't you let my wife say something? I don't think she ought to be thrust into the background like this.

MRS. LUNN. I'm sorry, I'm sure. Please excuse me, dear.

MRS. JUNO [thoughtfully] I don't know what to say. I must think over it. I have always been rather severe on this sort of thing; but when it came to the point I didn't behave as I thought I should behave. I didn't intend to be wicked; but somehow or other, Nature, or whatever you choose to call it, didn't take much notice of my intentions. [Gregory instinctively seeks her hand and presses it]. And I really did think, Tops, that I was the only woman in the world for you.

JUNO [cheerfully] Oh, that's all right, my precious. Mrs. Lunn thought she was the only woman in the world for him.

GREGORY [reflectively] So she is, in a sort of a way.

JUNO [flaring up] And so is my wife. Don't you set up to be a better husband than I am; for you're not. I've owned I'm wrong. You haven't.

MRS. LUNN. Are you sorry, Gregory?

GREGORY [perplexed] Sorry?

MRS. LUNN. Yes, sorry. I think it's time for you to say you're sorry, and to make friends with Mr. Juno before we all dine together.

GREGORY. Seraphita: I promised my mother--

MRS. JUNO [involuntarily] Oh, bother your mother! [Recovering herself] I beg your pardon.

GREGORY. A promise is a promise. I can't tell a deliberate lie. I know I ought to be sorry; but the flat fact is that I'm not sorry. I find that in this business, somehow or other, there is a disastrous separation between my moral principles and my conduct.

JUNO. There's nothing disastrous about it. It doesn't matter about your principles if your conduct is all right.

GREGORY. Bosh! It doesn't matter about your principles if your conduct is all right.

JUNO. But your conduct isn't all right; and my principles are.

GREGORY. What's the good of your principles being right if they won't work?

JUNO. They WILL work, sir, if you exercise self-sacrifice.

GREGORY. Oh yes: if, if, if. You know jolly well that self-sacrifice doesn't work either when you really want a thing. How much have you sacrificed yourself, pray?

MRS. LUNN. Oh, a great deal, Gregory. Don't be rude. Mr. Juno is a very nice man: he has been most attentive to me on the voyage.

GREGORY. And Mrs. Juno's a very nice woman. She oughtn't to be; but she is.

JUNO. Why oughtn't she to be a nice woman, pray?

GREGORY. I mean she oughtn't to be nice to me. And you oughtn't to be nice to my wife. And your wife oughtn't to like me. And my wife oughtn't to like you. And if they do, they oughtn't to go on liking us. And I oughtn't to like your wife; and you oughtn't to like mine; and if we do we oughtn't to go on liking them. But we do, all of us. We oughtn't; but we do.

JUNO. But, my dear boy, if we admit we are in the wrong where's the harm of it? We're not perfect; but as long as we keep the ideal before us--

GREGORY. How?

JUNO. By admitting we were wrong.

MRS. LUNN [springing up, out of patience, and pacing round the lounge intolerantly] Well, really, I must have my dinner. These two men, with their morality, and their promises to their mothers, and their admissions that they were wrong, and their sinning and suffering, and their going on at one another as if it meant anything, or as if it mattered, are getting on my nerves. [Stooping over the back of the chesterfield to address Mrs. Juno] If you will be so very good, my dear, as to take my sentimental husband off my hands occasionally, I shall be more than obliged to you: I'm sure you can stand more male sentimentality than I can. [Sweeping away to the fireplace] I, on my part, will do my best to amuse your excellent husband when you find him tiresome.

JUNO. I call this polyandry.

MRS. LUNN. I wish you wouldn't call innocent things by offensive names, Mr. Juno. What do you call your own conduct?

JUNO [rising] I tell you I have admitted--

    GREGORY {   } What's the good of keeping on at that?
    MRS. JUNO { together } Oh, not that again, please.
    MRS. LUNN {   } Tops: I'll scream if you say that again.

JUNO. Oh, well, if you won't listen to me--! [He sits down again].

MRS. JUNO. What is the position now exactly? [Mrs. Lunn shrugs her shoulders and gives up the conundrum. Gregory looks at Juno. Juno turns away his head huffily]. I mean, what are we going to do?

MRS. LUNN. What would you advise, Mr. Juno?

JUNO. I should advise you to divorce your husband.

MRS. LUNN. Do you want me to drag your wife into court and disgrace her?

JUNO. No: I forgot that. Excuse me; but for the moment I thought I was married to you.

GREGORY. I think we had better let bygones be bygones. [To Mrs. Juno, very tenderly] You will forgive me, won't you? Why should you let a moment's forgetfulness embitter all our future life?

MRS. JUNO. But it's Mrs. Lunn who has to forgive you.

GREGORY. Oh, dash it, I forgot. This is getting ridiculous.

MRS. LUNN. I'm getting hungry.

MRS. JUNO. Do you really mind, Mrs. Lunn?

MRS. LUNN. My dear Mrs. Juno, Gregory is one of those terribly uxorious men who ought to have ten wives. If any really nice woman will take him off my hands for a day or two occasionally, I shall be greatly obliged to her.

GREGORY. Seraphita: you cut me to the soul [he weeps].

MRs. LUNN. Serve you right! You'd think it quite proper if it cut me to the soul.

MRS. JUNO. Am I to take Sibthorpe off your hands too, Mrs. Lunn?

JUNO [rising] Do you suppose I'll allow this?

MRS. JUNO. You've admitted that you've done wrong, Tops. What's the use of your allowing or not allowing after that?

JUNO. I do not admit that I have done wrong. I admit that what I did was wrong.

GREGORY. Can you explain the distinction?

JUNO. It's quite plain to anyone but an imbecile. If you tell me I've done something wrong you insult me. But if you say that something that I did is wrong you simply raise a question of morals. I tell you flatly if you say I did anything wrong you will have to fight me. In fact I think we ought to fight anyhow. I don't particularly want to; but I feel that England expects us to.

GREGORY. I won't fight. If you beat me my wife would share my humiliation. If I beat you, she would sympathize with you and loathe me for my brutality.

MRS. LUNN. Not to mention that as we are human beings and not reindeer or barndoor fowl, if two men presumed to fight for us we couldn't decently ever speak to either of them again.

GREGORY. Besides, neither of us could beat the other, as we neither of us know how to fight. We should only blacken each other's eyes and make fools of ourselves.

JUNO. I don't admit that. Every Englishman can use his fists.

GREGORY. You're an Englishman. Can you use yours?

JUNO. I presume so: I never tried.

MRS. JUNO. You never told me you couldn't fight, Tops. I thought you were an accomplished boxer.

JUNO. My precious: I never gave you any ground for such a belief.

MRS. JUNO. You always talked as if it were a matter of course. You spoke with the greatest contempt of men who didn't kick other men downstairs.

JUNO. Well, I can't kick Mr. Lunn downstairs. We're on the ground floor.

MRS. JUNO. You could throw him into the harbor.

GREGORY. Do you want me to be thrown into the harbor?

MRS. JUNO. No: I only want to show Tops that he's making a ghastly fool of himself.

GREGORY [rising and prowling disgustedly between the chesterfield and the windows] We're all making fools of ourselves.

JUNO [following him] Well, if we're not to fight, I must insist at least on your never speaking to my wife again.

GREGORY. Does my speaking to your wife do you any harm?

JUNO. No. But it's the proper course to take. [Emphatically]. We MUST behave with some sort of decency.

MRS. LUNN. And are you never going to speak to me again, Mr. Juno?

JUNO. I'm prepared to promise never to do so. I think your husband has a right to demand that. Then if I speak to you after, it will not be his fault. It will be a breach of my promise; and I shall not attempt to defend my conduct.

GREGORY [facing him] I shall talk to your wife as often as she'll let me.

MRS. JUNO. I have no objection to your speaking to me, Mr. Lunn.

JUNO. Then I shall take steps.

GREGORY. What steps?

Juno. Steps. Measures. Proceedings. What steps as may seem advisable.

MRS. LUNN [to Mrs. Juno] Can your husband afford a scandal, Mrs. Juno?

MRS. JUNO. No.

MRS. LUNN. Neither can mine.

GREGORY. Mrs. Juno: I'm very sorry I let you in for all this. I don't know how it is that we contrive to make feelings like ours, which seems to me to be beautiful and sacred feelings, and which lead to such interesting and exciting adventures, end in vulgar squabbles and degrading scenes.

JUNO. I decline to admit that my conduct has been vulgar or degrading.

GREGORY. I promised--

JUNO. Look here, old chap: I don't say a word against your mother; and I'm sorry she's dead; but really, you know, most women are mothers; and they all die some time or other; yet that doesn't make them infallible authorities on morals, does it?

GREGORY. I was about to say so myself. Let me add that if you do things merely because you think some other fool expects you to do them, and he expects you to do them because he thinks you expect him to expect you to do them, it will end in everybody doing what nobody wants to do, which is in my opinion a silly state of things.

JUNO. Lunn: I love your wife; and that's all about it.

GREGORY. Juno: I love yours. What then?

JUNO. Clearly she must never see you again.

MRS. JUNO. Why not?

JUNO. Why not! My love: I'm surprised at you.

MRS. JUNO. Am I to speak only to men who dislike me?

JUNO. Yes: I think that is, properly speaking, a married woman's duty.

MRS. JUNO. Then I won't do it: that's flat. I like to be liked. I like to be loved. I want everyone round me to love me. I don't want to meet or speak to anyone who doesn't like me.

JUNO. But, my precious, this is the most horrible immorality.

MRS. LUNN. I don't intend to give up meeting you, Mr. Juno. You amuse me very much. I don't like being loved: it bores me. But I do like to be amused.

JUNO. I hope we shall meet very often. But I hope also we shall not defend our conduct.

MRS. JUNO [rising] This is unendurable. We've all been flirting. Need we go on footling about it?

JUNO [huffily] I don't know what you call footling--

MRS. JUNO [cutting him short] You do. You're footling. Mr. Lunn is footling. Can't we admit that we're human and have done with it?

JUNO. I have admitted it all along. I--

MRS. JUNO [almost screaming] Then stop footling.

The dinner gong sounds.

MRS. LUNN [rising] Thank heaven! Let's go in to dinner. Gregory: take in Mrs. Juno.

GREGORY. But surely I ought to take in our guest, and not my own wife.

MRS. LUNN. Well, Mrs. Juno is not your wife, is she?

GREGORY. Oh, of course: I beg your pardon. I'm hopelessly confused. [He offers his arm to Mrs. Juno, rather apprehensively].

MRS. JUNO. You seem quite afraid of me [she takes his arm].

GREGORY. I am. I simply adore you. [They go out together; and as they pass through the door he turns and says in a ringing voice to the other couple] I have said to Mrs. Juno that I simply adore her. [He takes her out defiantly].

MRS. LUNN [calling after him] Yes, dear. She's a darling. [To Juno] Now, Sibthorpe.

JUNO [giving her his arm gallantly] You have called me Sibthorpe! Thank you. I think Lunn's conduct fully justifies me in allowing you to do it.

MRS. LUNN. Yes: I think you may let yourself go now.

JUNO. Seraphita: I worship you beyond expression.

MRS. LUNN. Sibthorpe: you amuse me beyond description. Come. [They go in to dinner together].

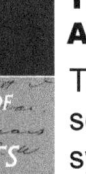

The Codes Of Hammurabi And Moses
W. W. Davies

QTY

The discovery of the Hammurabi Code is one of the greatest achievements of archaeology, and is of paramount interest, not only to the student of the Bible, but also to all those interested in ancient history...

Religion ISBN: *1-59462-338-4* **Pages:132**
MSRP $12.95

The Theory of Moral Sentiments
Adam Smith

QTY

This work from 1749. contains original theories of conscience amd moral judgment and it is the foundation for systemof morals.

Philosophy ISBN: *1-59462-777-0* **Pages:536**
MSRP $19.95

Jessica's First Prayer
Hesba Stretton

QTY

In a screened and secluded corner of one of the many railway-bridges which span the streets of London there could be seen a few years ago, from five o'clock every morning until half past eight, a tidily set-out coffee-stall, consisting of a trestle and board, upon which stood two large tin cans, with a small fire of charcoal burning under each so as to keep the coffee boiling during the early hours of the morning when the work-people were thronging into the city on their way to their daily toil...

Childrens ISBN: *1-59462-373-2* **Pages:84**
MSRP $9.95

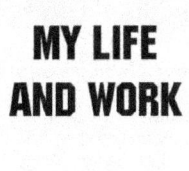

My Life and Work
Henry Ford

QTY

Henry Ford revolutionized the world with his implementation of mass production for the Model T automobile. Gain valuable business insight into his life and work with his own auto-biography... "We have only started on our development of our country we have not as yet, with all our talk of wonderful progress, done more than scratch the surface. The progress has been wonderful enough but..."

Biographies/ ISBN: *1-59462-198-5* **Pages:300**
MSRP $21.95

www.bookjungle.com *email: sales@bookjungle.com fax: 630-214-0564 mail: Book Jungle PO Box 2226 Champaign, IL 61825*

The Art of Cross-Examination
Francis Wellman

QTY

I presume it is the experience of every author, after his first book is published upon an important subject, to be almost overwhelmed with a wealth of ideas and illustrations which could readily have been included in his book, and which to his own mind, at least, seem to make a second edition inevitable. Such certainly was the case with me; and when the first edition had reached its sixth impression in five months, I rejoiced to learn that it seemed to my publishers that the book had met with a sufficiently favorable reception to justify a second and considerably enlarged edition. ...

Pages:412

Reference   ISBN: *1-59462-647-2*   *MSRP $19.95*

On the Duty of Civil Disobedience
Henry David Thoreau

QTY

Thoreau wrote his famous essay, On the Duty of Civil Disobedience, as a protest against an unjust but popular war and the immoral but popular institution of slave-owning. He did more than write—he declined to pay his taxes,   and was hauled off to gaol in consequence. Who can say how much this refusal of his hastened the end of the war and of slavery ?

Law   ISBN: *1-59462-747-9*   **Pages:48**

MSRP $7.45

Dream Psychology Psychoanalysis for Beginners
Sigmund Freud

QTY

Sigmund Freud, born Sigismund Schlomo Freud (May 6, 1856 - September 23, 1939), was a Jewish-Austrian neurologist and psychiatrist who co-founded the psychoanalytic school of psychology. Freud is best known for his theories of the unconscious mind, especially involving the mechanism of repression; his redefinition of sexual desire as mobile and directed towards a wide variety of objects; and his therapeutic techniques, especially his understanding of transference in the therapeutic relationship and the presumed value of dreams as sources of insight into unconscious desires.

Pages:196

Psychology   ISBN: *1-59462-905-6*   *MSRP $15.45*

The Miracle of Right Thought
Orison Swett Marden

QTY

Believe with all of your heart that you will do what you were made to do. When the mind has once formed the habit of holding cheerful, happy, prosperous pictures, it will not be easy to form the opposite habit. It does not matter how improbable or how far away this realization may see, or how dark the prospects may be, if we visualize them as best we can, as vividly as possible, hold tenaciously to them and vigorously struggle to attain them, they will gradually become actualized, realized in the life. But a desire, a longing without endeavor, a yearning abandoned or held indifferently will vanish without realization.

Pages:360

Self Help   ISBN: *1-59462-644-8*   *MSRP $25.45*

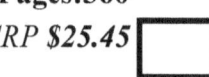

The Rosicrucian Cosmo-Conception Mystic Christianity by *Max Heindel*   ISBN: *1-59462-188-8*   **$38.95**
The Rosicrucian Cosmo-conception is not dogmatic, neither does it appeal to any other authority than the reason of the student. It is: not controversial, but is: sent forth in the, hope that it may help to clear...   New Age/Religion Pages 646

Abandonment To Divine Providence by *Jean-Pierre de Caussade*   ISBN: *1-59462-228-0*   **$25.95**
"The Rev. Jean Pierre de Caussade was one of the most remarkable spiritual writers of the Society of Jesus in France in the 18th Century. His death took place at Toulouse in 1751. His works have gone through many editions and have been republished...   Inspirational/Religion Pages 400

Mental Chemistry by *Charles Haanel*   ISBN: *1-59462-192-6*   **$23.95**
Mental Chemistry allows the change of material conditions by combining and appropriately utilizing the power of the mind. Much like applied chemistry creates something new and unique out of careful combinations of chemicals the mastery of mental chemistry...   New Age Pages 354

The Letters of Robert Browning and Elizabeth Barret Barrett 1845-1846 vol II   ISBN: *1-59462-193-4*   **$35.95**
by *Robert Browning* and *Elizabeth Barrett*   Biographies Pages 596

Gleanings In Genesis (volume I) by *Arthur W. Pink*   ISBN: *1-59462-130-6*   **$27.45**
Appropriately has Genesis been termed "the seed plot of the Bible" for in it we have, in germ form, almost all of the great doctrines which are afterwards fully developed in the books of Scripture which follow...   Religion/Inspirational Pages 420

The Master Key by *L. W. de Laurence*   ISBN: *1-59462-001-6*   **$30.95**
In no branch of human knowledge has there been a more lively increase of the spirit of research during the past few years than in the study of Psychology, Concentration and Mental Discipline. The requests for authentic lessons in Thought Control, Mental Discipline and...   New Age/Business Pages 422

The Lesser Key Of Solomon Goetia by *L. W. de Laurence*   ISBN: *1-59462-092-X*   **$9.95**
This translation of the first book of the "Lernegton" which is now for the first time made accessible to students of Talismanic Magic was done, after careful collation and edition, from numerous Ancient Manuscripts in Hebrew, Latin, and French...   New Age/Occult Pages 92

Rubaiyat Of Omar Khayyam by *Edward Fitzgerald*   ISBN:*1-59462-332-5*   **$13.95**
Edward Fitzgerald, whom the world has already learned, in spite of his own efforts to remain within the shadow of anonymity, to look upon as one of the rarest poets of the century, was born at Bredfield, in Suffolk, on the 31st of March, 1809. He was the third son of John Purcell...   Music Pages 172

Ancient Law by *Henry Maine*   ISBN: *1-59462-128-4*   **$29.95**
The chief object of the following pages is to indicate some of the earliest ideas of mankind, as they are reflected in Ancient Law, and to point out the relation of those ideas to modern thought.   Religion/History Pages 452

Far-Away Stories by *William J. Locke*   ISBN: *1-59462-129-2*   **$19.45**
"Good wine needs no bush,' but a collection of mixed vintages does. And this book is just such a collection. Some of the stories I do not want to remain buried for ever in the museum files of dead magazine-numbers an author's not unpardonable vanity..."   Fiction Pages 272

Life of David Crockett by *David Crockett*   ISBN: *1-59462-250-7*   **$27.45**
"Colonel David Crockett was one of the most remarkable men of the times in which he lived. Born in humble life, but gifted with a strong will, an indomitable courage, and unremitting perseverance...   Biographies/New Age Pages 424

Lip-Reading by *Edward Nitchie*   ISBN: *1-59462-206-X*   **$25.95**
Edward B. Nitchie, founder of the New York School for the Hard of Hearing, now the Nitchie School of Lip-Reading, Inc, wrote "LIP-READING Principles and Practice". The development and perfecting of this meritorious work on lip-reading was an undertaking...   How-to Pages 400

A Handbook of Suggestive Therapeutics, Applied Hypnotism, Psychic Science   ISBN: *1-59462-214-0*   **$24.95**
by *Henry Munro*   Health/New Age/Health/Self-help Pages 376

A Doll's House: and Two Other Plays by *Henrik Ibsen*   ISBN: *1-59462-112-8*   **$19.95**
Henrik Ibsen created this classic when in revolutionary 1848 Rome. Introducing some striking concepts in playwriting for the realist genre, this play has been studied the world over.   Fiction/Classics/Plays 308

The Light of Asia by *sir Edwin Arnold*   ISBN: *1-59462-204-3*   **$13.95**
In this poetic masterpiece, Edwin Arnold describes the life and teachings of Buddha. The man who was to become known as Buddha to the world was born as Prince Gautama of India but he rejected the worldly riches and abandoned the reigns of power when...   Religion/History/Biographies Pages 170

The Complete Works of Guy de Maupassant by *Guy de Maupassant*   ISBN: *1-59462-157-8*   **$16.95**
"For days and days, nights and nights, I had dreamed of that first kiss which was to consecrate our engagement, and I knew not on what spot I should put my lips..."   Fiction/Classics Pages 240

The Art of Cross-Examination by *Francis L. Wellman*   ISBN: *1-59462-309-0*   **$26.95**
Written by a renowned trial lawyer, Wellman imparts his experience and uses case studies to explain how to use psychology to extract desired information through questioning.   How-to/Science/Reference Pages 408

Answered or Unanswered? by *Louisa Vaughan*   ISBN: *1-59462-248-5*   **$10.95**
Miracles of Faith in China   Religion Pages 112

The Edinburgh Lectures on Mental Science (1909) by *Thomas*   ISBN: *1-59462-008-3*   **$11.95**
This book contains the substance of a course of lectures recently given by the writer in the Queen Street Hall, Edinburgh. Its purpose is to indicate the Natural Principles governing the relation between Mental Action and Material Conditions...   New Age/Psychology Pages 148

Ayesha by *H. Rider Haggard*   ISBN: *1-59462-301-5*   **$24.95**
Verily and indeed it is the unexpected that happens! Probably if there was one person upon the earth from whom the Editor of this, and of a certain previous history, did not expect to hear again...   Classics Pages 380

Ayala's Angel by *Anthony Trollope*   ISBN: *1-59462-352-X*   **$29.95**
The two girls were both pretty, but Lucy who was twenty-one who supposed to be simple and comparatively unattractive, whereas Ayala was credited, as her Bombwhat romantic name might show, with poetic charm and a taste for romance. Ayala when her father died was nineteen...   Fiction Pages 484

The American Commonwealth by *James Bryce*   ISBN: *1-59462-286-8*   **$34.45**
An interpretation of American democratic political theory. It examines political mechanics and society from the perspective of Scotsman James Bryce   Politics Pages 572

Stories of the Pilgrims by *Margaret P. Pumphrey*   ISBN: *1-59462-116-0*   **$17.95**
This book explores pilgrims religious oppression in England as well as their escape to Holland and eventual crossing to America on the Mayflower, and their early days in New England...   History Pages 268

QTY

The Fasting Cure *by Sinclair Upton*   ISBN: *1-59462-222-1*   **$13.95**
In the Cosmopolitan Magazine for May, 1910, and in the Contemporary Review (London) for April, 1910, I published an article dealing with my experi-
ences in fasting. I have written a great many magazine articles, but never one which attracted so much attention...   New Age/Self Help/Health Pages 164

Hebrew Astrology *by Sepharial*   ISBN: *1-59462-308-2*   **$13.45**
In these days of advanced thinking it is a matter of common observation that we have left many of the old landmarks behind and that we are now pressing
forward to greater heights and to a wider horizon than that which represented the mind-content of our progenitors...   Astrology Pages 144

Thought Vibration or The Law of Attraction in the Thought World   ISBN: *1-59462-127-6*   **$12.95**

by William Walker Atkinson   Psychology/Religion Pages 144

Optimism *by Helen Keller*   ISBN: *1-59462-108-X*   **$15.95**
Helen Keller was blind, deaf, and mute since 19 months old, yet famously learned how to overcome these handicaps, communicate with the world, and
spread her lectures promoting optimism. An inspiring read for everyone...   Biographies/Inspirational Pages 84

Sara Crewe *by Frances Burnett*   ISBN: *1-59462-360-0*   **$9.45**
In the first place, Miss Minchin lived in London. Her home was a large, dull, tall one, in a large, dull square, where all the houses were alike, and all the
sparrows were alike, and where all the door-knockers made the same heavy sound...   Childrens/Classic Pages 88

The Autobiography of Benjamin Franklin *by Benjamin Franklin*   ISBN: *1-59462-135-7*   **$24.95**
The Autobiography of Benjamin Franklin has probably been more extensively read than any other American historical work, and no other book of its kind
has had such ups and downs of fortune. Franklin lived for many years in England, where he was agent...   Biographies/History Pages 332

Name	
Email	
Telephone	
Address	
City, State ZIP	

☐ **Credit Card**   ☐ **Check / Money Order**

Credit Card Number	
Expiration Date	
Signature	

Please Mail to: Book Jungle
PO Box 2226
Champaign, IL 61825
or Fax to: 630-214-0564

ORDERING INFORMATION

web*: www.bookjungle.com*
email*: sales@bookjungle.com*
fax*: 630-214-0564*
mail*: Book Jungle PO Box 2226 Champaign, IL 61825*
or PayPal *to sales@bookjungle.com*

Please contact us for bulk discounts

DIRECT-ORDER TERMS

20% Discount if You Order
Two or More Books
Free Domestic Shipping!
Accepted: Master Card, Visa,
Discover, American Express